Words with Wings

Words with Wings

Nikki Grimes

WORDSONG
AN IMPRINT OF ASTRA BOOKS FOR YOUNG READERS
New York

Wordsong
An imprint of Astra Books for Young Readers,
a division of Astra Publishing House
astrapublishinghouse.com
Printed in the United States of America

ISBN: 978-1-59078-985-8 (hc)
ISBN: 978-1-63592-478-7 (pb)
ISBN: 978-1-62979-262-0 (eBook)
Library of Congress Control Number: 2013907720

First paperback edition, 2022

10 9 8 7 6 5 4 3 2 1

Design by Barbara Grzeslo
The text of this book is set in Bembo and Gill Sans.

For Elizabeth and Julia Bailey.
Don't let anyone clip your wings.

Contents

Prologue

Mom loves angels.
Their pink-cheeked faces
peek from pictures
on every wall
in every room.
So—surprise!
Mom decided to call me
Angel.
Dad said, "Enough already."
He didn't want his kid
named after some silly,
weak-looking chubby cherub.
He wanted
a strong name for his girl
to take out into the world.
Mom is stubborn, though.
She flipped through the Bible,
found a few fierce angels
and tried again.
"What about naming her
after Gabriel?
He was so fierce
people fainted
at the very sight of him."
That's all Dad
needed to hear.

Words with Wings

Two of a Kind

Mom calls me
Daddy's Girl
'cause him and me,
we're both dreamers.
"Close your eyes," he used to say.
"Tell me what you see."
I'd say, "Sky, shooting stars,
rainbows wrapped
round the earth."
"Now, it's my turn.
I see: you and me
bundled up in silver space suits,
bouncing on the moon.
Race you!" he'd say.
And we'd laugh,
back before he moved
across the street
and we moved
across the city.
Our laughter
has a lot farther
to travel now.

Summer Shift

We packed our bags in June.
I braced for a summer
of impossible good-byes,
and the dread
of living without friends
ever again.
To chase away the fear,
I flipped through a dictionary,
plucked out the word *hush*
and thought about
the whisper of wind
rustling through leaves,
come next autumn,
and the silence of their falling.
Then I jumped into
a soft deep pile of them,
grabbed an armful
of red, gold, and
burnt-orange beauties,

tossed them into the air,
and I was all right again,
for a while,
and I went back to packing
for the move.

Cheri

The kids at my last school
called me weird,
teased me,
or left me to myself.
Except for Cheri,
who picked me
to sit next to
in kindergarten
just because she saw me
staring out the window
and was dying to know
what made me smile
when all she saw
were raindrops.
I was shy about
telling her at first,
but Cheri didn't mind
my daydreaming.
She was color-blind, but said

whenever I described
my daydreams,
it was like
helping her see
the rainbow.

Hope

I hope this new school
has a Cheri who'll think
daydreamers are cool.

First Day

I duck down in the seat
of my new class.
To these kids,
I'm not Gabby yet.
I'm just Shy Girl
Who Lives
Inside Her Head.
No one even knocks
on the door
for a visit.
They don't know
it's beautiful
in here.

Gabby

One week in,
and already
my new teacher complains
about how much I daydream.
"Gabriella!" he'll say,
"Where have you gone off to
this time?"
I try to tell Mr. Spicer
it's not my fault.
Blame it on
the words.

Words with Wings

Some words
sit still on the page
holding a story steady.
Those words
never get me into trouble.
But other words have wings
that wake my daydreams.
They fly in,
silent as sunrise,
tickle my imagination,
and carry my thoughts away.
I can't help
but buckle up
for the ride!

Getting Started

Say "fly,"
and I go back to the
first daydream
that saved me.
I remember
there were screams,
a plate crashing
to the kitchen floor,
and angry words
ripping the air.
I pulled the pillow
over my head,
dove deeper under the covers.
Still, I could hear the awful sound
of their raised voices.
"Lalalalalala," I said aloud.
Still, I could hear them.
If only I could fly, I thought.
If I could fly, fly, fly away,
I'd go to the window,
step out on the ledge,
spread my wings and fly way
high above the city,
higher than the clouds.
I'd fly straight to Virginia,
fly to Great-Grandma's house.
I'd land on the porch,

hop on her swing,
and listen to her hum,
hum, humming to me.
And just then,
I could almost hear
Great-Grandma's hum,
could almost feel the gentle sway
of the porch swing.
And for a few moments,
I forgot
my parents fighting.
The word *fly*
had set me free,
and I wondered,
Are there other words
that can carry me away?

Gone

A few days later,
Dad packed his bags
and hugged me good-bye.
Something wet was in his eye
when he walked out the door.
I started missing him
that very second,
but I didn't cry. Instead,
I filled the quiet
with daydreams.

Concert

Say "concert,"
and I'm somewhere
in the past,
sprawled out on the grass
in Central Park,
my head cozy
in Mom's lap,
her head cozy
on Dad's shoulder.
I can't quite
make out the music,
but who cares?

Games

Say "Scrabble,"
and I'm giggling
next to Mom,
whispering words in her ear
while we gang up
against Dad.
He doesn't stand a chance,
but he grins anyway.
We come up with *QUIZ*,
beat him with a triple score,
and roar.
I sure do miss
those days with Dad.

Adjusting

It's been six months
and I still miss us,
the *us* that used to be
when Mom and Dad and me
were happy.
"Gabriella!" Mom calls.
"Please come and set the table."
I sigh and leave my memories
in my room.
"Coming!"

Setting the Table

I grab place mats
blue as the ribbon of sky
beyond my window
where pigeons invite me
outside to play.
But I've got a job to do,
so I shake my head no
and lay down
two knives and two forks.
When I fling a pair of napkins
toward the table,
one sails on the air
like a kite,
and I take off running
across the park,
chasing my crimson high flier
as it cuts across the blue
and—Mom asks me why
it's taking me so long
to set the table.
"Gabby! Snap out of it!" she says.
"I see you forgot the glasses.
Again."

Washing Dishes

Washing dishes,
I sink my hands into
rivers of soapy water
soft as sea foam.
I close my eyes
and float in the ocean,
sun warming my cheeks,
breeze tickling my skin
until Mom yells, "Gabby!
Stop daydreaming
and finish those dishes!"

Laundry

Mom runs to the store,
leaves me in the Laundromat
with a neighbor,
our clothes spinning
in the dryer.
I've seen pictures
of kids giggling in giant
whirling teacups,
and pretty soon I'm whirling, too,
hands raised to catch the wind,
dizzy with laughter,
which makes Mom groan
when she gets back because
the dryer stopped
when I wasn't looking
and I was supposed to be
folding clothes.

Report Card

At my old school,
all my report cards
ended the same:
Note:
Gabriella's mind
wanders.
I wonder why
they bothered
to write it down.
(Everybody
already knew.)
Will Mr. Spicer
write that, too?

Explain This, Please

Mom names me for a
creature with wings, then wonders
what makes my thoughts fly.

Nothing New

One or two hellos
greet me
at the classroom door.
I know not to expect more.
No one wants to be friends
with the weird girl.
I pass by rows of desks,
a make-believe grin
hiding my hurt.
Most days,
I'm an A+ pretender.
When I'm not,
I just crawl
into my daydreams
and disappear.

Arabesque

This weekend,
I stayed with my dad.
He bought tickets to the ballet
like I begged him to.
On the way home, he asked,
"So, what did you think?"
I closed my eyes:
I tied on my toe shoes,
checked the fit of my tutu,
then pirouetted and leaped
across the stage.
I pulled off a tight spin
and was about to leap again when—
"Gabriella? Where'd you go?"
I grabbed my dad's hand
and smiled.

A Trip to Thailand

Dad dreams out loud.
Once, he spun imaginary stories
about a trip to Thailand.
Mom waved off the idea,
said we didn't have
that kind of money.
Dad knew
she wasn't listening.
But, on his birthday,
Mom took him to
a Thai restaurant for dinner.
That's when he realized
she'd been paying attention
all along.

Mom's Complaint

Mom calls me to the kitchen,
a note from school
waving from one hand.
I stand in the doorjamb,
jumpy as a cat.
"Gabriella," she begins,
"what am I going to do with you?
You have to start paying
attention in school."
I gulp,
search my pockets
for some promise I can offer,
but only find the seashell
Cheri gave me
when we said good-bye.
"Did you hear me?" Mom asks.
I nod, finally breathing easy
when she sends me
to my room.

Maybe

Dad is a dreamer
and Mom is a maker.
I've been thinking,
maybe
I can be
both.

Sled

Say "sled,"
and my nose
is cold and shiny
as the blades
of the Red Racer I haul
to the top of the hill.
Then it's down

d
o
w
n
d
o
w
n
I
g
o

careening through
a lopsided snow fort,
waking the morning
with laughter,
steering straight into
the sun.

Snowflake

Say "snowflake,"
I start to shiver,
rip off my mitten
and giggle as one wet,
cold, lacy filigree
of winter white
falls onto my greedy palm,
then melts away.

Waterfall

Say "waterfall,"
and the dreary winter rain
outside my classroom window
turns to liquid thunder,
pounding into a clear pool
miles below,
and I can't wait
to dive in.

Mom

Mom watches me, sometimes.
I'll return from a daydream
and find her eyes
studying me.
Once, I asked her
what was wrong.
She shook her head.
"Nothing," she said.
"I—I wish I understood you better."
If only, I thought.
But I let her
go on staring.

Favorite Words

Mine: Pretend.
Mom's: Practical.
All we have in common
is the letter *P*.

Missing My Old School, My Old Life, My Old Family

Some days
sad is a word
I can't swallow.
It swells inside my throat
until it's stuck.
I hurry home from school
and beat Mom there.
The second she arrives,
I crawl onto her lap
like when I was little.
She holds me, quiet,
and strokes my hair.
I stay there
till the sadness shrinks
and I can breathe again.

Parent-Teacher Talk

I catch Mom
whispering on the phone
to Mr. Spicer.
I hear "new school"
and "hoped," "daydream"
and "stop."
Mr. Spicer must say
something like "don't worry"
because Mom says,
"You're right.
It doesn't help to worry,
anyway."
She hangs up the phone,
turns in my direction.
"Oh!" she says,
then smiles.
It's a nice smile,
but I still go to bed
feeling like
a problem.

Mom the Nurse

"I think your teacher,
Mr. Spicer,
is too easy on you,"
Mom says the next morning.
I study my breakfast bowl
to keep my thoughts
from flying out the window.
"What would happen
if I started daydreaming
when the doctor tells me
how much medicine to give
a patient, huh?"
"But I don't want to be a nurse,"
I say.
Mom rolls her eyes.
"I give up!"
I wish.

Wishful Thinking

I've figured it out:
Mom wants me to be
less like Dad,
more like she.

Teased

My week
doesn't get any better.
Jerome,
a bully-boy from my class,
bumps me,
sends my books sailing.
"Oops! Sorry!" he lies.
"Guess you were daydreaming, again.
Next time, watch where you're going."
I clench my teeth,
feel fire in my cheeks,
then tears come
to smother the flames.

Stuck in Dreamland

Maybe something
is wrong with me,
all this fancy dancing
in my mind.
Where I see red and purple
and bursts of blue,
everybody else sees
black and white.
Am I wrong?
Are they right?
Too bad
I can't ask Dad.

I Quit

I pack my daydreams,
kick them to a dark corner.
No more word-journeys for me,
seeing what others don't see.

Color-blind

On Monday
I shuffle to school,
eyes fixed on my footsteps,
no skipping ahead
on imaginary adventures.
I'm only me,
dodging broken whiskey bottles
in the street,
locked in the real, gray world
of now.

Perfect

I am perfect.
I stare straight
at the blackboard,
catch every single syllable
that falls from
Mr. Spicer's lips,
pass the pop quiz,
and still have
enough time left
to be bored.

Home Work

Girl robot,
I set the table stiffly,
but in record time.
After grace,
I count the peas on my plate
to keep my attention
on dinner.
For my next trick,
I slowly sip my milk,
avoiding conversation with Mom
who wants to know
how my day was.
"You're awfully quiet," she says.
I clear the dishes in answer,
scrub them till the squeak
can be heard on Mars.
"Homework," I say,
excusing myself
so I can disappear between
the colorless pages
of my workbook.

Correction

Mr. Spicer asks me
to stay after class.
I wait by his desk,
still as stone,
wondering what wrong thing
I've done now.
"Gabriella," he says,
"what happened to my dreamer?
I haven't seen her in days."
I shrug.
"She—I—gave up daydreaming
like everybody told me to.
Can I go now?"
Mr. Spicer sighs
and waves me away.
Good. I've got
nothing else to say.

Persistent

Teacher keeps an eye on me
all week.
I give him no reason
to call me aside,
but he does.
"Talk to me, Gabby," he says.
"Tell me what's wrong.
I can see you're not happy."
I'd argue but my sigh
gives me away.
"I miss daydreaming."
"Then daydream!" says Mr. Spicer,
confusing me.
"But you're always telling me
to *stop* daydreaming!
You and my mom."
Teacher taps his top lip
like a door the right words
are hiding behind.
"Dreams are great things, Gabby,"
he finally says.

"The best thinkers,
writers, inventors in the world
allow their thoughts
to carry them away,
now and then.
Take the Wright brothers.
We wouldn't have airplanes
if they hadn't dreamed of them, first.
Still, sometimes you have to
slide your daydreams
in a drawer
and let them wait until later,
like after I'm done
teaching a lesson
you need to learn.
Got it?"
I nod, wondering if
the Wright brothers
knew anything about
bringing daydreams in
for a landing.

Macaroni Memory

In the lunch line,
I take a deep, happy breath
and unlock the drawer
in my mind
where I'd been stuffing
all my daydreams.
"You can come out now,"
I whisper
and throw away the key.
Before I know it,
the word *Macaroni*
on the lunch menu
sends me to Daddy's kitchen.
He pours pasta into a pot
of ice-cold water
and I sigh.
"What?" he asks.
"You're supposed to
boil the water first," I tell him.
He smacks himself on the head,

switches off the stove,
and says, "Grab your jacket.
It's pizza time!"
I'm the first one
out the door.

Spring

Say "spring,"
and I am bouncing
on the balls of my feet
in a field of wildflowers
while April showers
tickle me
till I am slippery
as a snake
and soaked straight through.

Butterfly

Say "butterfly,"
and I am swimming in sunshine,
sprawled in the grass,
blowing on a blade
to make it whistle,
and eyeing the sky
for small, fluttering things
wearing rainbow wings.

Carousel

Say "carousel,"
and pale painted ponies
gallop past.
I reach for the reins of one,
swing up into the saddle,
and race,
standing still,
wind whipping my braids
as I fly.

Roller Coaster

Say "roller coaster,"
and I squeeze my eyes tight,
dig my fingers into
the safety bar
as we climb six stories,
then speed down again,
faster than my screams
can carry.
And as soon as we reach
the end of the ride,
I'm the first to yell,
"Do it again!
Do it again!"

Willow

There's this one kid, David,
plants himself in
the back of the room,
hair hanging over his desk
like a willow.
He talks even
less than me.
I wonder why.

Closer

One day,
I head in his direction,
pretend I need
to sharpen my pencil.
I manage to drop it
right next to his desk,
an excuse to bend down,
study him up close.
He hardly notices me.
He's too busy
drawing something
in his notebook.
Then, as I'm about to
grab my pencil and go,
his head pops up.
"Hi!" he says.
"You're the daydreamer!"
I nod, wait for some
nasty comment.

Instead, he grins golden.
"Cool!" he says.
That's when I know
I've found
another Cheri.

Switch

I use my sweet voice,
ask Mr. Spicer if I
may please change my seat.

Inside Joke

I clench my toes around
an imaginary tightrope,
then leap into
the safety net
just in time to catch
the question
Mr. Spicer throws.
"Gabriella, do you know
the answer?"
Sitting next to David,
I slide as low
as my chair will let me,
whisper, "Sorry,"
and try not to notice
Mr. Spicer
shaking his head.
A few minutes later,
David passes me his notebook.
I look down and see
Mr. Spicer staring back at me,

his hair a riot
of red, green, and purple pencil.
It's all I can do
to keep from laughing
out loud.

My New Best Friend

At recess,
David and I
swap cookies
and secrets.
He shows me his drawings.
I point to one sketch
of a clown.
"The circus is my
favorite place!" I say.
"Mine too!" says David.
He turns to a blank page
and starts sketching
a lion tamer.
Me? My thoughts trampoline
to the big top!

Stilts

Say "stilts,"
and I am
GABBY
THE
GREAT,
a mystifying
master
juggler,
rising
high above
the circus
crowd,
marching
alongside
the elegant
elephants,
and anxious
as anyone
to watch
the trapeze
artists
sail
on air.

Dragon

Say "dragon,"
and I raise my shield,
fend off the fire
of his mighty breath.
Then, when he's not looking,
I scramble onto his back,
grab a handful of scale,
and ride him across the sky
till the sun dives
into the sea.

Camp Dreams

The last snow just melted
and already
David is talking about
going to camp.
I ask Mom
if I can go, too.
Her "No" smacks me
in the ear.
"We have to count
our pennies," she says.
"Maybe next year."
I shrug, glad that the camp
in my memory
is free.

Tent

Say "tent,"
and I run my fingers
over the velvety moss
near my sleeping bag,
and I feel
the cool night air
ripple the hair
on my arms,
and I hear
the cricket chorus
while my cousins and I
melt marshmallows
and scarf down s'mores
round a campfire,
stuffing ourselves
with gooey goodness
under the stars.

Planetarium

David's mom
takes him on a trip
to the planetarium.
I know because
I get to go!
We lean back in our seats,
feel the dark wrap round us
like Saturn's rings,
and hold our breaths,
staring up at a night sky
speckled with starlight
and bigger than
all our dreams
slung together.
Can't wait to see
what drawings
David will do.
Me, I gather new words
like moon rocks,
souvenirs I get to keep
long after we leave.

Comet

Say "comet,"
and I am weightless,
playing ping-pong
with small planets,
dodging asteroids,
and skipping through space
in slow motion.
Two skips,
and I'm on the moon.
Two more,
and Mars
is my playground.

Teacher

Poor Mr. Spicer,
not sure what to do with this
dream/drawing duet.

Practice, Practice

I try to do what
Mr. Spicer said—
switch off my daydreams
during class,
save them for recess—
but my thoughts
have a mind
of their own.
Besides, the weather's
getting warmer,
and the trees
are whispering,
and who can concentrate
when the music
of the ice-cream truck
is right outside
the window?

Firefly

Say "firefly,"
and I close my eyes,
watch one wink
on and off,
an SOS
to gather its brothers.
Together, they rise and pulse
till I sweep them
into a jelly jar.
I tap the lid and grin
at my summer
night-light.

Sand

Say "sand,"
and I am running
along the beach,
snatching up shells
for my memory box,
Dad right beside me.
He oohs and ahhs
when I find
a beauty
and keeps his own eyes open
for sand dollars.
At the end
of the afternoon,
we trade treasures.
I smile and blink myself
back to the classroom.
For once, I write down
my daydream.
"I'll take that," says Mr. Spicer,
snatching the memory
right out of my hand.

Uh-oh

I.

David and I trade looks.
I wait for my punishment.
Mr. Spicer carries my paper
to his desk,
orders the class to
open their workbooks
while he reads
in silence.
A million moments later,
he looks up at me
with a smile.
I quit holding my breath,
but can't help
wondering why
he's not mad.
The lunch bell rings before
I can figure it out.

II.

David and I
worry together
over peanut butter
and jelly.
We share a cream-filled cookie
and I wash my half down
with a trickle of fear
and a cold carton
of milk.

Later

Mr. Spicer still hasn't
mentioned a thing
about my paper.
Even so, I make sure
to start the afternoon
eyes fixed on the blackboard.
I'm doing just fine till
the numbers begin to spin,
and the chalk draws
hopscotch lines
on the sidewalk,
inviting me to hop
from box to box,
balancing on one leg
like a ballerina
in sneakers,
and Mr. Spicer
doesn't even say a thing
to stop me.

Canyon

Say "canyon,"
and I am at
horizon's rim,
leaning over
a deep bowl of echoes.
I gape at the grand cavern
and call
"GABRIELLA!"
then wait
for the soft,
round sound of

ELLA!

E l l a!

e l l a!

as it returns.

Idea

"Gabriella,"
says Mr. Spicer.
"Didn't you hear the bell?"
I come back from my travels.
"Sorry," I whisper,
gathering my books to go.
"It's okay," he says.
"But before you go,
I have something to show you.
Remember this?"
He hands me the paper
he'd taken from me
earlier.
Here it comes, I'm thinking.
My punishment.
I slide down in my seat,
search for some way
to disappear.
"This was your daydream,
wasn't it?" he asks.
I nod, my tongue too tied
to answer.

"It's wonderfully vivid," he says.
"In fact, it's given me an idea.
I'll tell you all about it,
tomorrow.
That's it for today.
Go on home."
I leave
on giggly knees.
Now what?

Announcement

The next morning,
I race to school,
my mind too full of questions
to wander anywhere else.
I bounce up and down in my seat
while Mr. Spicer
takes ten times forever
to call the roll.
Then, finally,
"Class," says Mr. Spicer,
"starting tomorrow, we will
stop what we're doing
once a day
and daydream for fifteen minutes,
then write those daydreams down."
David looks at me,
his eyes wide as the moon.
"You'll never know when, though,"
continues Mr. Spicer.
"So you'll have to keep your eyes front
and pay attention.
Does that sound good?"

I swallow these words like honey,
smile at their sweetness,
and say, "Yes!"
my favorite word
of all.

Good Night

When class lets out,
I hurry home,
hungry for dinner
and hoping to find
more words with wings
to dream and write about
tomorrow.

Home

I kick my shoes off
at the door,
drop my books
on the kitchen table,
then hunt for snacks.
"Shoes in your room, please,"
says Mom.
I groan, but do exactly
what she tells me.
When I get back,
she's reading my paper!
The stupid page must've
slipped from my notebook.
I growl, then turn to leave
until Mom says,
"This is lovely, Gabriella.
I wish I could write like you."
What?
I slice up Mom's words
and nibble on them,

one at a time.
When I find my voice again,
I tell her all about
Mr. Spicer's plan
for our class.
"Good," she says,
smoothing my paper
like it's something—
precious.
If this is a daydream,
I don't want to know.

It's Here!

Tomorrow arrives
like a miracle.
Even so, the class creeps by
slow as the night
before Christmas.
I can't wait to open my
notebook and jot down
whatever daydream
comes to me.
I peek at David,
who shrugs in answer
to the question in my eyes:
When?
Finally, Mr. Spicer says,
"Okay. Class, workbooks shut.
It's daydream time."
I'm telling you,
I just about cry.

All In

Four weeks have passed
and my notebook is thick
with daydreams.
Funny how much better
I'm doing in school.
Somehow lessons don't seem
half as boring.
I'm not perfect, but
I hear most of what
Mr. Spicer teaches these days.
Plus homework's easier,
now that my mind's not
always meandering.
There's one more thing that's new:
My mom is starting
to daydream, too.

Author

Say "Gabriella,"
and Mom sees me,
silver-tipped pen in hand,
swirling "Best Wishes"
across the front pages
of dozens of books
with my name
printed on them.
I sign hundreds
round the clock
for a line of happy fans
that stretch a city block.
And there is Mom, beaming
right beside me.

Fair Is Fair

I never told Mom
I wanted to be a writer,
but I'll let her
keep her daydreams,
since she's finally
letting me
keep mine.

Acknowledgments

In the creation of every book, there are always particular people to thank for their encouragement, support, and inspiration. *Words with Wings* is no different.

I'd like to thank editor Rebecca Davis for encouraging me to expand the original picture book manuscript into a novel. Thanks to Amy Malskeit, who read and critiqued the manuscript while balancing a newborn baby girl on her hip. (Thanks, Lucie, for lending me your mom!) Thanks to agent Elizabeth Harding. I couldn't ask for a more enthusiastic fan.

I save my most heartfelt thanks for teacher Ed Spicer, who served as model for the teacher in my story. Ed regularly honors and nurtures the daydreamers who pass through his classroom by allowing them time to dream, and to capture their daydreams on paper. That was an inspiration to me and helped in the shaping of this story. It only seemed fitting to name my character after him. Thanks, Mr. Spicer!